UNDERSHIRTS
and other stories

Cathy Cockrell

Hanging Loose Press

Some of these stories first appeared in *Hanging Loose*.

Hanging Loose Press wishes to thank the National Endowment for the Arts for a grant in support of the publication of this book.

Published by Hanging Loose Press
231 Wyckoff Street
Brooklyn, New York 11217

Cover art and drawings by Robin Tewes

Thanks to Chaia, Chuck, Robin and Rose

Library of Congress Cataloging in Publication Data
Cockrell, Cathy, 1951 —

    Undershirts and other stories.

    Contents: Turquoise Wool Sweater, Fruit of the Loom Athletic Undershirts, Blue Work Overalls, etc.

    I. Title.

PS3553.029C57   813'.54   82-6073
ISBN 0-914610-30-9   AACR2

Produced at The Print Center, Inc., Box 1050, Brooklyn, N.Y., 11202, a non-profit printing facility for literary and arts-related publications. Funded by The New York State Council on the Arts and the National Endowment for the Arts.

To Myrriah

CONTENTS

Turquoise Wool Sweater

In need of a good cleaning, it hangs in the closet under my loft bed. In the days when it belonged to Marilyn Morris, I doubt it ever needed cleaning. Marilyn had only a few orderly, elegant possessions there at the top of Mr. Boorady's converted brownstone. Barbara and I lived in the apartment under hers and above an old woman, no more than a shadow on the ground-level floor.

Both Barbara and I are prone to collecting things, and in this place, at the time, under those conditions, our possessions were plentiful but shabby. We took a trip to the Salvation Army in her taped-together car to assemble a life from the discardings of others—plated aluminum, plastic, things half-used and half-broken for the kitchen; a mattress not really wide enough for two; a lesbian porn novel "for fun"; a worn copy of *Mary Poppins* for the curt, enchanting, and untouchable heroine so much like, I kept on thinking, the roommate who read it aloud to me at night. There was dried vomit on the floor near the window when we moved in, which Barbara scrubbed till it came clean. Still, one could never scrub out the memory of it, registered with every sense.

If we had succeeded in getting a room at The Harmony, a populated, quirky rooming house nearby, we would not have had to scrub vomit—though there were other things: the Harmony landlady told us, in a low voice, about the tenant who incinerated her "monthlies" in her kitchen stove. "Hush!" Some sort of hush prevailed, too, in Mr. Boorady's with Marilyn, someone who seemed as permanently in the environment she relentlessly perfected as we, beneath, were temporary in ours, a creature spinning out of herself the sparkling and ordered web she inhabited. She had flushed cheeks and sturdy, hand-woven baskets and healthy plants; her laughs were soft as balls of cashmere yarn. Evenings she knitted colored wool sweaters, the turquoise one among them, affixing seven yarn flowers in a circle on the front—burgundy, purple, black. This sweater virtually sang from the corner of the room where it lived, folded, or from Marilyn's body as she came up the building's dull stairway or down the street. A flat, smooth seam along the inner wrist finishes the sleeve; more perfect seams run along the shoulder and the yoke where the ribbed turtleneck joins the rest.

Once Marilyn wore it on the stoop, transferring a houseplant from a pot that had broken. And the sweater, bright as my turquoise birthstone, declared itself to me at the far end of the block, heading home from work. Tired, tormented, in some ways miserable with our graceless, confusing life, I moved toward a symbol of perfection. One day, unexpectedly, she would give it to me. She would move across country with a boyfriend who visited in a Dodge van. Mr. Boorady crusaded against "fornication" on the premises, so they slept together in the Dodge, which the paperboy began referring to as the "get-it-on-van."

On our bed by the window, near the scrubbed vomit, Barbara and I lay and touched each other—wrong sometimes, sometimes right—doing something we had no name for, confused, tentative, denying and isolated. We knew no one. Except, I should say, my boss Sam. Barbara worked for the Arthur Murray Dance Studio as a telephone solicitor, peddling cha-cha lessons, and I worked for Sam, a stringy, independent, and impractical man. Sam and I fixed furniture during the day and I remember nighttimes when we varnished cabinets under the dim light and high ceiling of his workshop. There were silences between us, awkwardness, longings as we pulled the varnish along the grain of wood with our fine-bristled brushes, eliminating bubbles and seams.

Later, at home, I would deliberate over each day's interactions, his inflections, possible meanings. And Barbara, listening or seeming to, never said a whole lot. She never spoke her whole mind about it, I could tell, when we finished our odd dinners and our chipped dishes, when we read the night's chapter about outspoken Mary Poppins, when we lay so frightened between the sheets, incapable of words, while Marilyn, in the get-it-on-van, folded the turquoise sweater.

Fruit of the Loom Athletic Undershirts

Washed and folded athletic undershirts, stacked on open shelves, offer fantasies and facts of you, them, us and me, skin and shoulder blades and bone, angles of flesh and dominance, control and freedom. On city streets, July middays, men sit on milk crates, eating lunch and drinking. With particles of sweat caught along their brows, in faded denim jeans and white athletic undershirts, they talk; wear their vulnerable weapons pressing the insides of their pants; claim the space stretching from this leg to that, spread wide. They stand, sit, curse and shout and shove, bear hidden miniature piles of colored fruit on the label flat against each neck, give a recognizable form to the formlessness of athletic undershirts. They claim the space stretching from this knee to that, spread wide, and the rectangles of pavement where women pass rapidly, eyes averted.

Running vertically from the yoke below their neck chains to the bottom machine-stitched edge below the waist are high, then low, ridges of cotton along whose parallels the body carves shapes of youth and power. We wear these undershirts too—either boldly, barely hiding our breasts, or prudently, under other shirts. Your silver labyris on the delicate chain falls near the shirt's top edge; the vertical ribs

15

follow the contours of your breasts, your bones, your solid, muscular body. By the end of the day, or the next, depending on humidity and heat, the shirt will stretch, lose tone, fall away in places where it once hugged close and comforting. Then it must be thrown into a limp heap with the others, unuseable, until their next journey through the suds, water, and heat of the laundry, the motion of your hands flicking and folding, smoothing and stacking the still-warm white shells, thin garments trailing streams of meaning and desire like the misty veils of teenage brides.

At the local laundromat, where we did our clothes together, the brand of detergent flakes became a contest of wills. You refused the box I'd bought on sale, would use only the particular brand you've sworn by for years. Later we cooperated, pooling our dimes to get everything dry. And I watched, aware, catching details suffused with meaning: the way the hair pushed back from your brow and temples, the sinews visible in your neck, nothing extra between your bones and skin. Hauntingly androgynous, unique but universal, you were the promise of something undefined and inaccessible I wanted and awaited as you handled your Fruit of the Loom shirts with a care that should have told me, from the onset, of their importance in our wardrobe of possibilities.

On the laundromat's public counter you took a long time folding the undershirts, denim bell bottoms, soft worn work shirts. Then we stacked our double load into the squealywheeled cart. Later, once we got it home, we would climb into your fresh sheets, our limbs tangled, fingers tentative, filling our hands with each other's bare breasts, or not—you grew reluctant to shed the undershirt, the power and protection of that last thin molt before the skin.

"It's OK," I'd keep on telling you, being the accommodator, paralyzed in my fear to push back, to know you naked, equal, bare of the vestments of importance and toughness you choose, I clothe you in to make you larger, powerful. I don't remember you asking about my life. You were telling stories about your past, times I need and needed to imagine, years when I was still new in the world, in tiny child's oxfords. While you, a seventeen-year-old, would go to the dance hall, you tell me, decked out in a suit, brimmed felt hat and blue suede shoes. We look at photos of Paula, a femme in a tafeta gown and nearly twenty years your elder, who leaned toward you at the door to ask: "Kid, you wearin' your father's shoes?" You nearly fell off your feet, you say. You describe the proportions of your humiliation.

You were passionately in love with Paula, or about to be, you've told me. And I've entered that time, that emotion. Late into the night we sit up in bed, eating cookies from the box between us, thumbing through the photo album, as you point things out: Paula seated at the edge of the dance floor, tipping a beer bottle; you in your sharp suit, doing the lindy. One night in a dream she turned to you and said "You're the best friend I've ever had." You shuddered as you told me in the morning, wondering at the distance that forever separated you two, despite your two-year affair; what she made of you; whether she's still alive. Your eyes follow the curve of her skirt against the chair. "Some of us," you say, "are afraid to wear our dresses." And I look, stalking significance. But you've shut the book. You reach and turn off the light. My hands touch your back through the night, reading your vertebrae for affection.

Or I hold the fierce lavender dragon tattoo, high on your thigh, the tattoo discussed by your various ex-lovers at parties all that year we spent together. I supposed you knew this when you walked in, to a hero's welcome, the sisters screaming hellos across the room to you, a superdyke among us. We greeted each other against the wall, for that moment shy and cautious with each other. I was wearing a formal tux, a

17

bow tie, and a blue carnation, my hair combed back like Elvis —an outfit that seemed almost to astound you. You literally fell back a step, I thought, as if I grew close and blurry; as if crowded by new facts, and their wild shadows, truth. Asking me "Wherever did you get that idea?" Though it clearly is an old one, older by far than you.

We took a winding staircase to the apartment's overhanging second floor, do you recall, where the woman in the "Come Out!" t-shirt cut cocaine into lines on a mirror. We were aware of each other; our affair was new then; there was a wildness in us. We started throwing underwear from the chest of drawers over the railing, as if the party upstairs were really getting hot, and socks still in pairs in wide, high arcs onto the women dancing below. Then women began stripping and you ripped off your shirt. And my startling tux came off—it felt like freedom and a submission to you, both— and the leather boots. Underneath I wore girls' socks, the undershirt, my panties. "Just lucky," you told me, playing naked cop: two articles of women's clothing were required by law, or I would have been thrown in jail. I could feel one of your tales of the old days coming on.

Women came to tell you goodbye at the door as we left the party. We walked home slowly through the streets, singing silly songs:

> A sailor went to sea sea sea
> To see what he could see see see
> But all that he could see see see
> Was the bottom of the deep blue sea.

I know that sailor. You have described him to me. He had grey eyes—steel grey and thoughtful. He gave you money. You knew what you'd have to give him in return. But with him you were surprised: all he wanted was to offer up his worries, things he'd seen that he needed to tell on solid

18

ground, objects steady around him. "Your money or your life," they say. He gave you both. The bills were in the drawer beside the bed and he kept talking, in his pants and socks.

This life being crazy, I recognize this story. And will hear it again and again, till the night turns thick. And then, if you must, you just keep on talking, to the wall. I—or someone else I recognize—will be there sleeping, one arm thrown around you, fingers searching the ridges and furrows of your undershirt, covering your breasts.

Blue Work Overalls

I step into these blue work overalls and chant it, a mantra: "'Are you a boy or a girl?' he said. 'I see,' he said. 'I see,' he said, looking down."

And remember this: The summer in Seattle is bright and hopeful. The boasted September-through-May Rain Festival is over and sun reflects from the bridge where the suicides jump, winters, raising the city's notorious rate. It reflects from the aluminum corrugations of Lake Union's thousand boat houses, from the fiberglass bellies of the Chris Crafts, from the plate glass windows of marina offices facing onto the lake. It heats our winches, barrels, rough piers, the Wallbangers' houseboat, the part cotton, part polyester fibers of the blue overalls, stitched with my name, that the industrial clothing outfit brings each fortnight, taking the second pair to be laundered. The legs hang straight and loose. The company had to shorten them considerably for me, and I wondered if anyone else could ever be fitted in them. But it didn't work that way: eventually, when I quit, I haggled the company's truck driver down from $7.00 to $4.00 for the things. Knowing somehow that they would prove forever useful for car repairs, painting, and to answer the question (marked with my female name): "Are you a boy or a girl?"

Harvey Wallbanger was the name of the drunk who asked the question. The name my boss Art gave him for those evenings just home from Happy Hour when he stumbled out of his big white Oldsmobile and down the slatted pier to his fiberglass houseboat and his aging, waiting wife.

Harvey was more than a sot; he was mean-spirited, too. I knew, and at the same time did not know, the type as if by reflex, like my own breath, my face, the lines in my palms. His old white head was grandfatherly, to my eyes. So that it felt disconcerting, but familiar to me—not knowing his real name: I never could remember my own grandfather's first name either. I was three when he died. His last name, the one leading back through the generations of fathers, was York. "Duke of York," I would think. "English," I concluded. And remembered a question I'd once heard asked by a feminist historian: "What is England without its colonies but a rock with some asparagus and flowers and springtime?" By way of my mother's stories grandfather York was my idea of a bad rock in a distant place: bleak, unyielding, hard. Redeemed and humanized by women. He came from the Bad Lands, South Dakota, and moved as a child to Chicago. Older, visiting southern Illinois one summer, he seemed a star from the metropolis in the eyes of a farm girl, my grandmother Clara. The brilliance of lightning in the close, knotted sky above the farm. Civilization, promise, the one man in the world not in overalls.

Clara was good-hearted, I was told, and never confident about her pies. "But her yeast breads!" my mother would say, rolling her eyes toward heaven. I saw her photo under the glass on my mother's bureau. She died in her sleep when I was four. She had a plain cotton dress and an impressively full bosom. I imagined her as bounteous as it was. I imagined her repelled and also attracted by my grandfather, a handsome man who seldom spoke to her. He played favorites to his son, my uncle Kenneth, a man I've never known. He stacked coins by little Ken's bed and cursed his daughter, a thick nuisance moving below his kneecaps.

Playing sandbox as a child and still, years later, scraping barnacles from a boat propeller, I sifted and resifted all the bits of things I knew about the world, examined and re-examined shapes and surfaces to imagine persons, events, the remote lost causes for so fierce and particular a hate for women. And my grandmother: what drew her to him, made and kept her the long-suffering Mrs. York? I know I asked the winches, the barrels, the rocking pleasure cruisers, the dirty impenetrable lake. I asked my boss and the surly mechanic, by observing them, and Harvey and his wife when I saw them. Harvey's wife, by association with Harvey and possibly in her own right, was named Mrs. Wallbanger. Daytimes she stayed alone in the houseboat in its covered slip— puttering inside, spraying the deck, cleaning the plastic flowers. We would wave hello to each other as I passed.

Once, just once, we talked. It must have been spring at the time. The rain festival was on. A light slanting rain was catching my feet and cuffs, weighing them down, and Art was away buying parts. So I took up her offer, stepping away from the pier, and sat a few minutes in the cabin of her houseboat. She gave me hot tea in a plastic cup and spoke pleasantries, searching out at me from the eyes of a woman adrift—ones that surprised me, yet ones I recognized as my own. I was twenty and had ended up somehow back in my home town after a bout of California crashpads, crummy jobs, sordid sexual encounters and a big jilting by a boy I thought was Jesus. Anti-war marches up the Seattle freeway only three years before had been ten thousand strong and I had been in them and still remembered and longed for that particular, exciting relation to history. The issues out there were still as oceanic, but I existed in a different, more difficult relation to them, caught in my own and the time's confusions, a tidepool with a compelling, seemingly deadly force of its own.

I would tell you the color of Mrs. Wallbanger's eyes that day, the shape of her cheeks, the thickness or thinness of her lips and how her voice moved through the houseboat's chilly galley. But all these things that now have importance I do not remember. I was still down under, sunk in thoughts or perhaps not thoughts but the weighted feeling that overcame me during my three-hour bouts of work in the bowels of the pleasure cruisers, as removed from outside stimuli as a deep sea diver in a dark and motionless tank, or Mrs. Wallbanger in her home.

Later I would want to reconstruct her features and her story, to know what she and Harvey saw in each other as young lovers and who had given up what to live on board. Harvey Wallbanger would have already stood above me in the marina parking lot saying "Are you a boy or a girl?" as I leaned over the handlebars of my bicycle, ready to ride home, and the snapped blue front of the overalls hung away from my body and Harvey, peering down in, would say "I see. You're a girl." And I, humiliated, would wish the disgusting sot dead. I would remember, and keep remembering it later that summer when the Oldsmobile stood unlocked and unused and Harvey Wallbanger's one buddy called the marina to check up on him at which point an unopened bag of groceries was found in their galley. Then both Harvey and Mrs. Wallbanger were found missing and a day later Harvey's body was dredged up by the harbor police from the bottom of the lake under their houseboat.

Mrs. Wallbanger was never found by the dredging hooks. So that how she managed to leave and where she might be lingered in my mind mornings, fiberglassing a deck, afternoons painting some cabin down below a glossy white, my blue overalls getting spattered and my head spacing out on the fumes and my troubles. I crawled up into the sunlight, at long last, one afternoon to see Art, his finger pressed against the nozzle of a hose, spraying away the revolting smell of her body that they had laid up on the dock. The mechanic had discovered it floating under the main pier, mistaking her at first in the silent dim space for a log.

I craved to know so many things; to see her, even in her state, one last time; to know if she had considered herself happy and if this was an end she wanted; to reconstruct the events; to feel their shape and weight and meaning. But her body had already been covered and carted away. The last of the officials had left. The reporters, even, had come and gone. I bicycled home that afternoon, the day's sun warm against the seamless blue back of my overalls, my mind burning with its questions.

Cotton Polka Dotted Skirt

The skirt hung at home those months in 1942. It hung in her closets through a war, a wedding, a move west, the house building, and the children's growing up.

In 1970, at nineteen, I take it from its hanger and put it in the backpack along with other essentials—the jeans, magic markers, a paperback copy of *The Electric Koolaid Acid Test*. I am heading for California where the hippy women wear cotton skirts and ankle bracelets. Where they pass the acid test of these strange times, the book says, on a bus called "Onwards," on the bunk beds squirming with a thousand sperm, on Ken Kesey's ranch up Old La Honda Road. The book says the Pranksters put speakers in the trees there to broadcast lunatic babblings as the doors of consciousness are opened by the acid punch and Kesey, the high priest, plays his harmonica. You know you've found the ranch, the book says, when you hear the notes drifting through the foliage.

Like Kesey, like cowboys at night, I have the harmonica. Like the pioneer and hippy women, and like my mother, I wear the cotton skirt. She wore it in the halls of a big city highschool. Chicago in the '40s. It moved around her calves, blue rickrack, like miniature waves, nipping at the hem. Its yellow and blue dots on the white background, each marked with thin black lines and a circle, resembled plankton, microbes, or other common, minute things that swim in the universe. She wore it with cotton blouses like any highschool girl in those days studying history, geometry, and biology. Its gathered material fell in folds beneath the desk as she held the colored pencils tightly, in her fury, drawing meticulous diagrams of microbes, worms, the fetal pig. She labored to locate the parts that ingest, digest, expel and those that register the creature's living and its dying pain. She drew a thin straight line from each membrane, cavity, and organ to its label.

Not merely because of the teacher's assignment but by intuition she felt the importance of these names—how the hope of any control over her pinched and injured life was in this act—like the search to name and so to conquer what she learned and lived in her father's house under his fierce and well-aimed hatred. She learned, among other things, that the heart which is said to break is not unique among the internal organs. One day in 1942 her appendix swelled with poison and her mother put her in the hospital. But her father, when he learned, would have none of it. Not all that money—on his daughter! He removed her from the hospital; the sac burst at home. As a child I saw her standing naked near the bathtub and I reached up to feel the scar, near the top of the pubic hair, where the surgeons entered, too late. The poison, spreading, had inflamed the membrane lining the walls of the abdominal cavity. "Peritonitis." This time she stayed in the hospital six months, waiting for the infection to end.

Now it is 1970 yet still "the 60s." I wear the skirt on ramps, thumbing rides into San Francisco, to Mendicino, to Baja California. I ride with the surgical equipment salesman, the hippies, the Anaheim Satanists, the minister, the race car driver. I step off the curb into his low-slung silver car, heading for "the city." We cross the hills to take the coast highway. We wind along a road none other than Old La Honda Road. I am looking through the rain and wipers for the signs of the ranch where the Prankster men, as priests, reveal another, better, reality through the sorcery of acid. I am straining for the hawonk of Kesey's small musical instrument.

My own harmonica rests on my lap, nested between the folds of microbe-dotted cotton. The hem falls to my sandalled feet. I feel the light weight of the material on my skin as we toke grass by the roadside, half-way over the hills, rain clouding the windshield. There is a particular gravitation in the car that changes, as if shifting to a higher gear. The race car driver makes a pass and I pretend not to notice. Finding the harmonica on my lap, I begin the first tune that comes to my head: "What a Friend We Have in Jesus." The driver puts his hand to my breast. I already know the story of what is happening to me: I know that next it will be my thighs, my cunt. I am dazed, yet a struggle is on between us. He bruises the flesh near my hipbone as I try to push him away. The harmonica goes flying across the car.

Instinctively I begin to demand his name. Over and over, as he presses against me through my clothes, I say "What's your name?" "What's your name?" I say. "Tell me your name!" Finally he tells me: "Bill." And I use it as a weapon, making human contact. "Let me out, Bill!" I tell him. "Stop it, Bill, let me out!" Under the mysterious threat of it he even rescues the harmonica for me, between his seat and door, and hands it over as I lean in the open door on my side, my daypack in hand, ready to move.

In a slackened rain he drives on up the hill. I walk back down Old La Honda Road, drizzle soaking my feet, my hair, the skirt, and all its water-loving microbes. I hawonk rough tunes on the harmonica, look back behind me at each bend, feel my bruised flesh for scars.

33

Chinese Silk Blouse

In the dark of my closet my fingers locate the Chinese silk blouse by its elaborately textured yoke. They unfasten, then fasten on me, its cloth-covered buttons; read the exquisite braille of Chinese garment workers' needlework, from the shoulders to the last cluster of embroidered circles between my breasts and navel. I know, too, by heart the faint stain at the hem, the one that Pritti made one December, disturbed by thoughts of home.

I run the edge of my hand across the blouse at the lower back, parallel to the floor. This gesture stands for the long, thick blue-black hair that fell there. I never saw Pritti groom it, only heard her brush pulling through it in the dark, like I never saw her dress or undress in the college dorm room we shared, only saw her gather clothes in preparation for her trip to the bathroom each morning on rising and each night before bed. There was speculation among a few of us, her friends, as to the source of Pritti's modesty. Some believed it was purely personal. Some were sure it had to do with India, at least in part—didn't we remember Pritti saying how strictly moral her grandmother and her aunts were, and how she cursed words like "Backwards!" out loud as she read airgrams from her relatives back home?

I got a small idea of the way Pritti should behave when she took me Thanksgiving vacation to a Hindu temple in Washington, D.C. She wore a sari, for the first and only time all year, and the erect dignity I understood differently there than I had on the campus. Inside the dimly lit temple Pritti took a place before a statue of Krishna that was set into a recess in the wall and decorated with peacock feathers and flowers. From the moment she sat down something came over her: her hands in her lap were still as waterlillies in a quiet, sunstruck pond; words in another language came naturally from her lips, which barely moved. Her manner, as she sat there and when she got up, seemed to make a strong impression on the priest: he nodded, spoke to her at the door, and smiled as if charmed by whatever it was she said in reply, speaking Hindi. It has been strictly to mollify the priest, a friend of her father's, she giggled afterwards. I giggled too, believing.

It had been hot the day in late August when we arrived separately on the college campus—Pritti and I both wilted from long flights. At room assignment I was given my dorm, my floor. When I came to the door my roommate-to-be was already there, a foreign, dark-skinned woman with exceptionally long black hair. It appeared that she had claimed the bottom of the bunk beds: her suitcase lay open on it, with photos of a man in western suit and turban, women in saris, lined up against the suitcase divider. I felt annoyed that she had chosen her bed unilaterally. Then she said "You prefer the upper bed?"

"I do," I said truthfully. I was relieved to find that my roommate might not, in fact, be impossible. We introduced ourselves. I dropped my things inside the door, sighed deeply, and observed her. She wore a long skirt, sandals, an antique off-white short sleeved blouse. Its embroidered front reminded me of a great aunt of mine I met once, and had seen in photographs, always in smocked dresses she made by hand. My great aunt's had been cotton, Pritti's was of silk. Its back sparkled in the sunlight as she set carved wooden animals along the window sill and chipped away at a prior student's candle drippings where she apparently felt the bird carving belonged. Books, clothes, photographs, and nicknacks she arranged with deliberateness, then helped me organize the side of the room that would be mine.

Later that night, from our bunk beds, Pritti and I could hear the wisteria pods crack open on their woody vines outside the window. I held very still, so as not to squeak the springs. I wanted to hear the wisteria and the crickets and to hear Pritti's breathing below me. I wondered if she would talk. I was afraid she'd simply fall asleep. I asked where the photographs were taken.

"Of my family?"

"I think so. The man in the suit? The women?"

"My father," she said. "My mother and aunts. Those were taken in Delhi. I consider it my home."

"What do you mean?"

"Where I live, when I'm not here." Her tone was sharp.

"I meant what did you mean by 'I *consider* it my home.'"

"Oh. That I've lived a lot of places—France, Trinidad, other places."

"Really!" I said, waiting for her to explain. Maybe her father was a rich businessman who set up foreign subsidiaries.

She contradicted my thoughts: "My father works for the Indian government. He's a diplomat." She reminded me about the blouse she'd worn that day. "It came from China. One of his trips."

"Did you like that—moving around?"

"It was acceptable." I pictured her arranging the carvings so carefully on the sill. "And you?" she asked.

"I consider the west coast my home, if that's what you mean."

"You've lived other places?"

"No. Just there."

She wanted to know why I had come east to college. That was a hard one. "Some idea about culture," I speculated. She didn't say anything, like she was trying to comprehend it. I was going to have to explain something I didn't understand myself.

"For a lot of Americans, my parents for example, culture is in the east."

"The American culture is in the east?"

"Yes. Well not 'the American culture.' But 'culture' to some Americans, if you understand the difference I'm driving at. You know: symphony orchestras, great art museums, dance, theatre, old wealth. You understand what I mean by 'old wealth?'"

"Are you kidding? India!" she exclaimed, as if that said it all. "Princes and rhajputs! Imperial harems! The Taj Mahal!"

"This thing about culture, it's sort of dumb," I defended myself, aware of the reproach and excitement in her voice. But when Pritti wanted to know something she was relentless.

"Your ancestors," she quizzed, "where are they from?"

"Europe somewhere. Then the Midwest. I did once meet one of my grandparents' generation—Great Aunt Sciota, my mother's mother's sister. She ran the farm in southern Illinois where she and my grandmother and their brothers had grown up. She flew out to visit once when I was quite small." I could feel Pritti really listening. As if my fractured, partial understanding of my family past, the information and the holes in the information, could help her understand America. As if, putting that together with what she already knew—including five languages and at least three cultures—she would understand the world.

With reluctance and, I think, relief, I told her the haphazard things she coaxed from me, that I'd never told an

American: that the nights were hot on my mother's summer trips "down home" to the farm. That my grandfather, a railroad accountant, stayed at home in Chicago, figuring with severe precision what had been gained and what must meagerly be given. While his wife and daughter, gladdened with relief, left behind the harrowing marriage, the city torpor, the job at Marshall Fields. They rode the lines south into the heartland, their bags bulging with gifts—towels and sheets and pillow cases grandmother sold in the big store's linen department.

"You visited the farm?" Pritti's voice asked.

"Not in person," I told her, trying to be patient; I thought I'd said that already.

"What do you mean?"

"I mean only indirectly, through my mother's stories. I got a picture of the place that way. Though I never really paid attention to the details, or the way she told it, until lately. Not to be able to retell it, I mean."

"And," Pritti said, not asked, as if terribly annoyed to be kept waiting. Maybe being an Indian diplomat's daughter was like being a princess.

"My mother always talked about the heat," I told her. "That was the big thing. And a willow tree that grew near the farmhouse. On the south side. Every midday, when it was hottest, my grandmother, mother, uncle, and whoever else was there—*that* I don't remember," I put in, as if really holding my ground—"would collapse under the tree. Fanning themselves with paper fans in its shade. Fanning, talking, waiting for the inevitable sound of the screen door. My mother would describe the exact kind of creak the door made as it opened, then shut, and Sciota approaching, always in one of the white dresses with smocked bodices. And what it felt like as she came, like a presence almost more than someone they only saw: Sciota bringing a tray of juice pressed from arbor grapes, each glass tinkling with cubes of ice, each sweet and cold and wet—a heaven, the way she told it." I wondered if that story seemed random and pointless to Pritti or if she understood why it got told and retold. "I guess it's the idea of a place in time where my mother remembers safety, love, community," I philosophized.

"Yes," Pritti answered, in a tone that reproached me for presuming to explain. Or was it for the sentiment itself, some idea about the past which Pritti could not condone?

"My grandmother, also, brought us drinks to cool us," she told me.

"Lassi," I volunteered, half asking, half exclaiming the name of the one Indian beverage I knew. I informed her, since she seemed so interested in America, that Lassi to Americans was a television collie associated with June Lockhardt and Campbell's Soup.

"Not Lassi," she stopped me, repronouncing the word with a softer 'a.' "Flavored syrups mixed with ice water and milk. They're very popular in India. And very, very old."

"Fruit flavors?"

"Yes. Cherry. Strawberry. And others you might not expect—sandalwood, other things," she alluded. We had come to the end of that. Or so I thought. But Pritti meant for me to understand I should not speak frivolously of India. Behind the syrups were the centuries.

"You've heard of the Moghuls?"

I asked her to repeat it.

"Moghuls. You've heard of Ghengis Khan?"

"Yes. He was very, very brutal, wasn't he?" I had once seen an old Hollywood film about him on tv. I remember he sat in a big chair and ordered beheadings.

"Ghengis Khan was a Moghul," she said firmly. "They were Moslem invaders."

"India was invaded?"

"Yes. Afghans, Turks, the Moghuls. The Moghul rulers established a series of capitals, some with huge mosques, in the north of India. One day Akbar the Great or one of them got thirsty and hot. He ordered men to bring him ice from the Himalayas to the north. It was done. The flavorings were added and the sherbets invented. We drink them still."

"That's good," I told her, liking the story.

"I'm told it happened something like that," she answered.

"Aaah," I said, and if Pritti meant for me to be impressed with the history weighing upon those syrups, she succeeded. Her voice brought news of the past, which I experienced almost physically, as a kind of gravity in which Pritti below me, was grounded. While I, though attracted, was beyond its reach.

As she had explained the syrups I had heard in Pritti's voice a masked but ferocious pride. Now I heard it dissolve and shift, suddenly and as if unprovoked. I heard raw exasperation, another curse at India. She was talking to herself.

I can see her, pensive and alone, as we sang Christmas carols in the college lounge—strange tunes to a boy-God we imagined pale in his manger. We all raised our paper cups of wine for a toast. Then Pritti's, her fingers firm around it, rose even with the rest. The cups were all identical, yet I was aware of which rim among them belonged to hers, and oddly conscious of the time and place: December in America.

"Merry Christmas," we said, tapping cups together. Pritti's lips moved too, and quietly she said the words, then began to drink the purple wine as we did. But she faltered, and it missed her mouth, spilling instead down her front. Desperately she watched the color spread as a sophomore versed in home remedies hurriedly poured salt over the front of the blouse, lifting out the entire stain except for a small indefinite shape that remains today.

The day classes ended for the year Pritti was wearing a

polo shirt and jeans I'd given her. The antique blouse I had admired all year was laying on my desk, where she'd put it. I should wear the old thing for the summer, she told me gruffly. Only later would I realize what I think even then, somewhere, she knew—that she wasn't coming back.

"Transferred," the registrar told me, in a voice intended to reassure, when I asked after Pritti the following September. Her name had simply been dropped from the list of returning sophomores. It was then I realized how much I had counted on seeing her again, all our cautions and distances notwithstanding. All that fall and spring I felt her absence and for years afterward, whenever and for whatever reason I felt loss, Pritti would reappear in my dreams.

As for what became of her, whether she finished at an Indian university, and what manner of peace she made with India, these are questions that persisted and persist, like those I asked and ask about Great Aunt Sciota. Even in the dark, eyes blinded, these women can be located, and by the strangest means: any filled suitcase I chance to see; the faint stain of spilled wine on a blouse's hem; needlework on its white silk yoke crafted long ago somewhere in China. I feel the texture of the threads its makers painstakingly located, drew apart, built up, removed—the residue of lives, a fabulous design.

Blue Navy Sweater

What is essential is not the dark, eventless front, the plain long sleeves ending in a standard cuff. It is not the ribbed bottom or the round neck itself, but the small label sewn inside the neck that reads "Carl" in simple black letters. What is essential is that a long time back it belonged to my uncle, the Methodist minister my father calls affectionately "the fat friar."

My father had kept the sweater unused in his drawer until I got my hands on it and kept it, because it had been Uncle Carl's. Old troubles had clouded everything I might have known about it, or Carl, or how my father had gotten it—troubles beginning with my grandfather and his broher, two YMCA men who became contenders for a prized directorship. It was just at that time that my father was implicated in a local scandal—the theft of a collection of trophies from the Y's display cases. My grandfather's brother was given the job; it was something for which my father would be blamed and not forgiven. He enlisted in the army, there was a war on anyway. When the war was over he resettled far away from them so that, between the distance and the strained relations, he had little contact anymore with his family and any knowledge of them became obscured and inaccessible to me until the day, at twenty-eight, when I visited the fat friar—my first contact with any of my father's two brothers or three sisters in my adult life.

I rode the Greyhound up, on a night run, wearing the Navy sweater. A snowstorm caught us on the way. The passengers were slumped in their seats along the thin, dark aisle, sleeping. From the front seat opposite the driver I watched the lighted dials on the dash and the white storm swirling out of nowhere all around us, blurring everything.

I couldn't sleep. I bunched the sweater cuffs into my fingers to keep warm. I kept wondering about them all. My cousin Beverly, Carl's daughter, had told me a little. She had turned up one day, out of the blue, at my apartment. She saw my anti-nuke leaflets and told me about her own affinity group and how her father approved. She didn't say anything about the lesbian posters. She nodded when I told her I am the outcast in my family.

A week after her visit I got an invitation in the mail from Uncle Carl, ending with the promise that we would discuss the problems of "this nuclear, hungry world." But I wasn't going to talk about the end of the world. If he started in on that I meant to change the subject to the color of my father's socks as a child or the photo albums where I might search the faces for some explanations, clues to my father's past, for the missing links between my life and the human stories up-river, so to speak, in time.

Uncle Carl did talk of nukes, it turned out, but of some other things as well. We saw old slides. I saw the fat friar in the house in Madison long before the fat accumulated and before the divinity degree. I saw my father's brothers on their return from the last world war. I saw Carl on the porch steps of the old house, blowing the bugle in his blue sweater as he had on Enewetak Atoll in the South Pacific. His unit was sent to the island following the bombings of Hiroshima and Naga-

saki, staying till the summer day of 1946 when the Navy bull-
dozed its planes and trucks off the end of the island and
shipped the boys home, to begin its A-bomb testing there.

When Carl got home he unpacked the Navy sweater from
his duffle bag and sported it around campus and to the greasy
spoon near the state capital where he worked as a short order
cook. He must have taken some care there—no stains of food
or indelible grease are left to immortalize the joint.

The last day of my visit, a Sunday, my reverend uncle
preached from the pulpit, in ministerial robes, against the
authority of parents. He told the story of "The Prodigal Son"
—better named, he said, "The Forgiving Father," the father
who awaited and welcomed back the errant child. All the
while as he spoke he looked the spitting image of my own
father, raising the prayer book over those familiar eyes in
ritual motions, offering us bread, from the altar, in the name
of God. Between the lines he was sending messages to my
cousin Beverly, she later confided, concerning the fact he had
only recently learned—that Beverly had been caught at school
smoking marijuana.

After church she and I put on borrowed equipment and
skied through a graveyard and up the side of a small moun-
tain. The snow storm had ended the night before and already
people had made tracks we could follow down. The day was
sunny and warm. We peeled off layers in the graveyard at the
bottom. My parka, gloves, and the blue sweater rested on top
of a stiff bush as we took photographs in someone's family
plot, between the headstones.

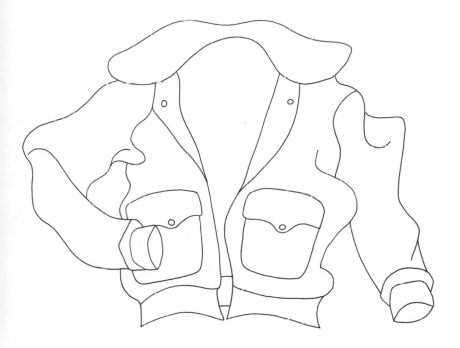

Khaki Bomber Jacket

I remember it was hot out the day I arrived in Berkeley and that I sweated under the jacket, but how I kept it on. At the time that made some peculiar sense. Even then there was something elusive yet compelling about the jacket: a history of human terrors imbedded in the fibers or between that skin and the imitation fur lining. Besides, nothing then was making run-of-the-mill sense. At anti-war demonstrations I had been to in the three years since I had been seventeen men with bull-horns had yelled "What do we want?" and I had never known whether my honest answer was "Peace!" with half the crowd or "Revolution!" with the other. Another thing you heard was "be here now"; but I was a failure at that, thorned with memory.

I would remember finding the jacket in my father's base-ment trunk or would imagine the man wearing the jacket in the world war. I've always believed he was an Airforce pilot and a friend of my father, since it ended up in our house. I assume he was a slight man, since the coat fits me. Up the front there's a copper-colored zipper; around the neck, a gold fur collar. The fur, though imitation, feels like a quiet animal friend, perched up there, protecting. The skin is cotton, smooth from wear. Small stitches hold together a torn place on the left sleeve.

This jacket, I imagine, kept the pilot warm inside the cold airborne craft he piloted, on order, the collar circling his neck as the bombardier's voice, in his ear, signalled that the bombs were away, dropping onto Dresden. It was February, 1945. The pilot knew his terror bombing aimed to shatter German morale; he had not heard of Churchill's desire to impress Stalin with U.S. airpower as the war with Germany came to an end and the Big Three discussed the future of Eastern Europe. His earphones were built into the sides of his khaki-colored cloth helmet, the kind I was to find among the household military relics, the kind my father would hook up to the television when I was a child. My brother and sister would sit before the television wearing the cloth helmets, long cords leading from the backs of the hats into the rear of the set. In this way they could watch "Twentieth Century," sponsored by Prudential, while I practiced piano behind them. I saw Auschwitz, Hiroshima, and Dresden out of one eye as I played tunes, in C:

> We went to the zoo
> To see the noisy crew
> The lion jumped out of his cage
> And chased the kangaroo.

I saw filmclips of land and air invasions. Fascinated, I watched parachuters floating as if weightlessly, midair, robbed even of the assurance of gravity sucking one at great speed toward disaster.

I recognize that sense of suspension. I remember travelling through that time in which I came of age. I remember hitchhiking with a friend Larry and the ride we got from some people travelling to an anti-war demonstration. At Fort Ord, on the California coast, we saw the place where future soldiers shot at targets in the sand. We piled out of the car, onto the road, where a massive contingent of uniformed policemen waited. We blocked traffic into the base, chanting

"Bring the War Home!" We answered the man with the bull-horn and when the police charged we ran. The sleeve got torn in the fracas and still bears the stitched scar to commemorate the protest.

Then Larry and I were in another car, with some of the protestors who had come from Berkeley. When we got there Larry said he wanted to hang out awhile in the Bay Area. He was tired of hitchhiking and hassles. His parting gesture was a casual wave; his final words some lyrics that drifted back to me as he left: "You who are on the road, must have a code . . ." —a song he'd meowed, hummed, and chewed all the way from Eugene to Mexico and back.

The snatch of song was some piddly solace to me. I was disoriented and hassled. Maybe it was the street vendors with their jewelry, leather, and roach clips spread on scraps of velvet near the campus, maybe the messages on the CoOp bulletin board I read for rides and kicks. Like this, under "Housing": "Looking for that vague sense of community . . ."

On University, the main drag out of town, I stuffed the jacket inside my pack and sat against a building. I would look for a hitching partner and a ride north. I waited a long while before I saw the guy come down the curb flashing a sign at passing cars. The back side of the cardboard read "North," the other "South." I figured, considering the looseness of his plans, that he might consider a partner. He did. Little crows' feet crinkled out from the corners of his eyes. He had a weak but friendly smile, a small pack, a smooth leather jacket. His name was Brian. He'd been a GI in Nam. He understood what we each had to gain from a partnership: I'd feel safer than having to stand alone, again and again, on the freeways between Berkeley and Eugene; he'd get rides faster, being with a woman.

It wasn't long till a VW bus stopped for us, its destination northern California, way up by the Oregon border. Happy, we crawled in. The back seats had been removed. We sprawled on a foam mattress. Sun and pot filled the air inside the bus as we road north through the long day. I lay on my back, feet against the rear panel, my head propped on my gear. I saw the flat fields out the window. I watched the long, arching spray from the irrigation sprinklers, beads of water falling like silver bullets. The driver and his front seat companion talked behind me, making spacey, incomprehensible comments all ending with the question "You know?" I didn't know. I knew I was tired. I knew I was on my guard. I knew I couldn't let go till I reached Eugene.

At Mt. Shasta the driver let us out. Brian and I went for the on-ramp and stuck our thumbs out again. With a little bit of luck we might be offered a ride into Oregon, where hitchhiking was legal even on the highways. With *great* luck someone would stop and take me all the way into Eugene that night. Just beyond us was a posted sign saying "No Hitchhiking Beyond This Point." I read the messages on the back of it scrawled by previous hitchhikers: "Shasta Sucks," "2 Days' Wait," "Hijacking is Faster." It reminded me of all the discouraging things I'd heard about hitchhiking out of those conservative northern California towns. Pick-up trucks with mounted gun racks sped past on the on-ramp, diesel trucks thundered along the freeway as we watched night ease down around us.

Eventually we gave up, beating a way through underbrush beside the road. A powerful yellow-green light, mounted above a gas station, helped us stake out a patch of ground. I folded my jacket into a pillow and got into my sleeping bag. Brian spread out my rain slicker and lay down on it. He lit a cigarette and I stared at its glowing end, an orange star under a stationary yellow-green moon. The night, though cold and clean, felt awkward, dangerous, and wrong. To be a rodent, I thought; to burrow and stop my senses. I drew the inner sur-

56

face of my sleeping bag in close against the sound of crickets in the grass, sixteen-wheelers on the freeway, Brian's shivers and his restless rubbing and beating at his jeans to warm himself. I heard him say my name, his voice rising and moving towards me. "I'm freezing," he said. I had hoped his leather coat would keep him warm enough.

He had to struggle to squeeze into my sleeping bag. His coat was thick and heavy next to me. I gathered in the top of the stretched and gaping bag again as best I could. I was on my side; he was curled around my back, his body pressed hard against me. I was startled but not surprised when his arm moved around my body, searching for my breasts. I told him "don't." His hand moved down my stomach, still searching, kneading my flesh like an angry baker. "Don't" I said again, my voice small and desperate. I felt his strong arm fixed around me, then felt him hesitate, and felt it pull away.

"No," he said, just audibly. "I haven't come to that."

Say something—anything! I told myself. But he talked first, changing the subject.

"My bag got ripped off in El Paso. All my shit was in these people's car. I go inside a joint to buy us hamburgers. When I come out, no car, no shit. We'd ridden together four days."

"Weird" was all I could manage.

"I ate enough hamburgers and fries to choke a horse."

Then there was a long silence between us, while a shrill cricket somewhere nearby screamed murder in my ear. Out of nowhere Brian said something: "Dong Ha." He was in a place called Dong Ha. I felt an emotion ripple through him. I wished I could fling off my paralysis and the bag. I held on.

"What's Dong Ha?" I said. "Why is this place Dong Ha?"

He began telling about his mission to Dong Ha, near the DMZ. A medical evacuation—his first and last. "From Danang. To collect and airlift the wounded and dead GIs. You load

57

the living onto litters, put the dead—the really mangled ones —into plastic body bags. Tag 'em and ship 'em home—Detroit, Georgia, the Bronx. The place was still under VC fire. Christ! A 'copter was hit midair while I was down there. Exploded into flames and came down. I couldn't begin to guess how long we were in there or how many guys we found or how many DOAs came in. I went out for a last guy I thought I heard, moaning like anything. I went for him, in some brush, and then I don't know—I got separated. There was a lot of fire coming down and I couldn't find that motherfucker and I just couldn't make it back either. At one point I heard them scream for me. They didn't hear me yell back—they took me for dead. And then I heard them take off. I was alone. I spent two days and nights there, not moving a muscle, afraid the Cong would spot me. There were snakes."

The fibers of the sleeping bag twisted treacherously around my body. The sky was mean and cold and distant above the ragtag encampment of our two bodies. I saw one ugly star flickering in it, as if it would go out for good, abandoning me to this GI and all the rest: the diesel trucks rumbling on the interstate were mortar fire; the yellow-green light was a helicopter burning midair; the rednecks were Cong. I smelled his jacket, its strange scent of processing, and felt the collar of my own prickling my cheek. I heard the Eighth Airborne pilot cussing his living brains out and swallowing hard in the sky over Dresden and heard the catch in Brian's voice and heard us again between the base and the ocean yelling "Bring the War Home!" I felt the constricted muscles in my throat. I felt Brian's knuckles, cold and hard like the grooved barrel of a revolver, pressing into my shoulder. I remembered the feel of my distant breasts and feet and cunt. And I knew for once I was being told something that I understood.

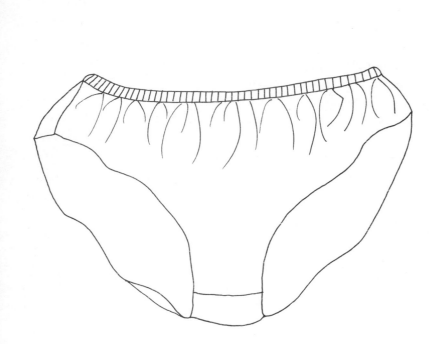

White Cotton Panties

You say you want to shed last night's smell of sex and sin. You want to leave your yellow terrycloth panties here in my apartment. You want to borrow a pair of mine. You laugh when I hand you this pair of white panties with the tired elastic band. You say: "Now don't give me your very best!" They're the last of the Pima Princesses I buy at Penney's girls' department whenever I go home to Seattle.

You're unique. Other sisters say: "I'm attracted to you." You say: "Ooooo, baby, you're hot. I want to eat your pussy." You act wild, yet hold my thin body with exquisite tenderness. You tell me again of your hard times past, your furious past. In Brooklyn, the '50s and '60s: a time I shared, a distant place.

Sometimes I wonder: Will I ever understand about screwing with Tommy Saladino under the boardwalk? Or how a girl feels as he throws the wet rubber out into the Atlantic? I remember your snapshot of Tommy in the barracks, wearing the Valentine boxers' trunks you sent and I ask: did you give them casually, or with particular feeling for this first boy you'd let all the way inside you? Where were you when I spotted jellyfish in Elliott Bay, as a child, from the decks of ferryboats with Indian names? Where was I as you ran on short legs from the littered water at Chickenbone Beach, asking your daddy for the name of those flabby white floating creatures the Tommy Saladinos of the world had cast away? "Coney Island Whitefish" was a variety we never dreamed of when we held our small fishing rods from the rock wall at Alki. Our English is a different language.

By now I can picture some things about your Brooklyn childhood. I can see the men jerking off in the subway station tunnels as you came home from school, shuddering. I don't forget the horrible one who came in your pocket on the D train. Nor the men who entered, spreading your window gates, to take your stereo. Nor the one who murdered little girls in series.

But you know, don't you, that a small-time kook with his underwear collection has a shape and a weight, too, a sound and a smell, in the mind of a young girl, the memory of a woman? That a stranger's come in your pocket is not the only texture of "experience"? And that out of these, our separate pasts, things unexpectedly stir our memories, cause one of us to sweat, trip on her tongue, laugh, flush, turn crazy or sad remembering. And it may be a subway tunnel or a girl's vulnerable pocket on the train. Or it may be some simple panties you jokingly call my "best"—plain white ones like the Seattle girls wore, like the panty man collected and stored in the caverns of our children's world, our labyrinth tunnels, our chambers and crawlways in a woods where children still could play without risking death. We only risked the possibility of one day coming upon a lone man with a compulsion to break and enter houses in our part of the city, stealing girls' underwear, women's lingerie.

The summer the panty man hit town, the summer I was nine, we turned the place we called "The Big Woods" into a labyrinth of sticker patch rooms with connecting crawlways. We cut the juicy blackberry stalks near the ground, yanked at the severed and barbed vines, snaked them out of the tunnels. The tangled mass of discarded vines outside grew tall and brown as the maze inside grew more elaborate: tunnels leading to more tunnels, chambers connecting to others. Clear through to the room I liked the best where the layers of leaves made voluptuous shades of green laced with tiny points of light.

It was there in the farthest room, where the children's voices came through remote and dim, that I found him crouching among his stolen trophies—bras and underpants hanging all around him on the tiny sharp hooks of the blackberry thorns.

Why are you here in the Big Woods, my best room? I wanted to know. That man was grinning but he wasn't answering. My heart was pounding. Far behind him on the top surface I could see a single blackberry attached to a vine, its tiny pouches of juice all touching each other. I wanted to be outside picking it. Even if I had to lean over thorns to reach it. Even if the stickers made ragged scratches in my arms. To be standing free in the sunlight picking it! I thought the man would reach out for me, his arm brushing the white cup of a bra hanging from the walls. I imagined he would touch my nipple through my blouse as if it were a berry and he would pick it. My blackberry was miles away.

He is going to touch me all over, he is . . . No, I told myself. *He's only a sort of museum keeper. He only wants my panties for his collection. They will hang, snowy white, from a green hook under the sticker dome, next to the neighbors', all touching where his hands will touch . . . where his hands will touch.*

I found the man in our room and I knew he would touch me and fear held everything like a skin—then, and later that summer when the Seattle policemen came to get him, when their badges glinted outside the tunnel and the light revolved on the roof of their car like a throbbing sun. Standing on the pile of rotten brambles I saw the entrance choked with the blue of their uniforms as they dragged the panty man out of the tunnel, the white bras and panties draped over his arms like the pelts of little slain animals. I watched him hand his trophies to the policemen, felt the motion of his arms reachin out as I had seen them reach out for me. I saw his face and the policemen's faces as they passed the objects between them, like the rare, precious secrets of initiates. Believing—even they and then—in the Pima Princesses' talismanic powers, their connection with the mysteries of sex and sin.

Shall we, then, consider it ritual as I give you this garment on the morrow of our intimacy. Shall we take in the mysterious and unlikely crossing of our life paths in this old city, your home, eternally new to me. And measure how our longings, cavernous as empty subway stations, or gestures small as this, extend beyond the Hudson and the present. Shall we remember the masturbator's corner and the panty man's museum; appreciate our hands' motion exchanging underwear; recognize between us, women of the New World that we are, the geography of our common fears, the landscape that we both inhabit.